For Nicola (who continues to adapt well to the ways of Earth).
Thanks for everything. — S. B.

First U.S. edition 2002

Library of congress cataloging-in-Publication Data is available.

Library of congress catalog card Number 2002276817

ISBN 0-7636-1897-7

2 4 6 8 10 9 7 5 3 1

Printed in Belgium

This book was typeset in Bokka.
The illustrations were done in acrylic.

candlewick Press
2067 Massachusetts Avenue
cambridge, Massachusetts 02140

visit us at www.candlewick.com

Man on the Moon

(a day in the life of Bob)

Simon Bartram

CANDLEWICK PRESS

CAMBRIDGE, MASSACHUSETTS

THIS is **Bob**. Perhaps you've heard of him.
You may know him better as the **Man on the Moon**.

This is where Bob lives. Every morning he gets up at six o'clock. He has a cup of tea and two eggs for breakfast before leaving for the rocket launchpad. On the way he stops to buy a newspaper and some chocolate candies.

He's on his way to work . . .

. . . on the MOON!

By eight o'clock Bob arrives at the launchpad. He changes into his special Man-on-the-Moon suit and boards his fantastic rocket ship.

He has to make sure he leaves by quarter to nine, or he won't make it to the Moon by nine.

On the way he reads the newspaper and does the crossword puzzle.

Bob starts work. His job as Man on the Moon is very important. He has to keep the Moon clean and tidy. Quite often astronauts drop candy wrappers and cans.

Some people say that aliens are responsible for much of the trash, but Bob knows that's not true. There's no such thing as aliens.

By twelve-thirty it's time to eat.

Bob goes to his rocket ship to get his lunch box. Usually he eats two sandwiches (either cheese or peanut butter), an apple, and some chocolate-covered nuts.

Sometimes he meets his friends for a picnic. His two best friends are Billy, the Man on Mars, and Sam, the Man on Saturn. They talk about the stars and tell jokes.

After lunch, tourist spaceships start
arriving from Earth. It's part of Bob's
job to entertain the tourists and
give them something to photograph.

They seem to like somersaults, handstands, and especially high Moon jumps. Sometimes Bob performs for as long as two hours and gets quite out of breath.

Sometimes the tourists' spaceships will land on the Moon. When they do, Bob gives the tourists a guided tour and a speech. He tells them lots of facts, such as how many craters the Moon has, or how long it takes to walk around it on stilts.

Sometimes people ask him about aliens, and Bob explains patiently that there aren't any.

Afterward, Bob opens a small souvenir stand. He sells postcards, pens, coffee mugs, and small plastic Moon models.

By four-thirty all visitors
must leave the Moon. Bob looks
around to see that everyone has
left. He checks inside the big
craters in case someone has fallen in —
but there's **never** anyone there.

The working day is nearly over – it's time to check that everything is in order before leaving for the night. Bob packs his equipment and any unsold souvenirs into his rocket.

He switches on the Moon's night-light before jetting off toward Earth.

By this time he's very tired, but he still has to keep his wits about him while flying the rocket.

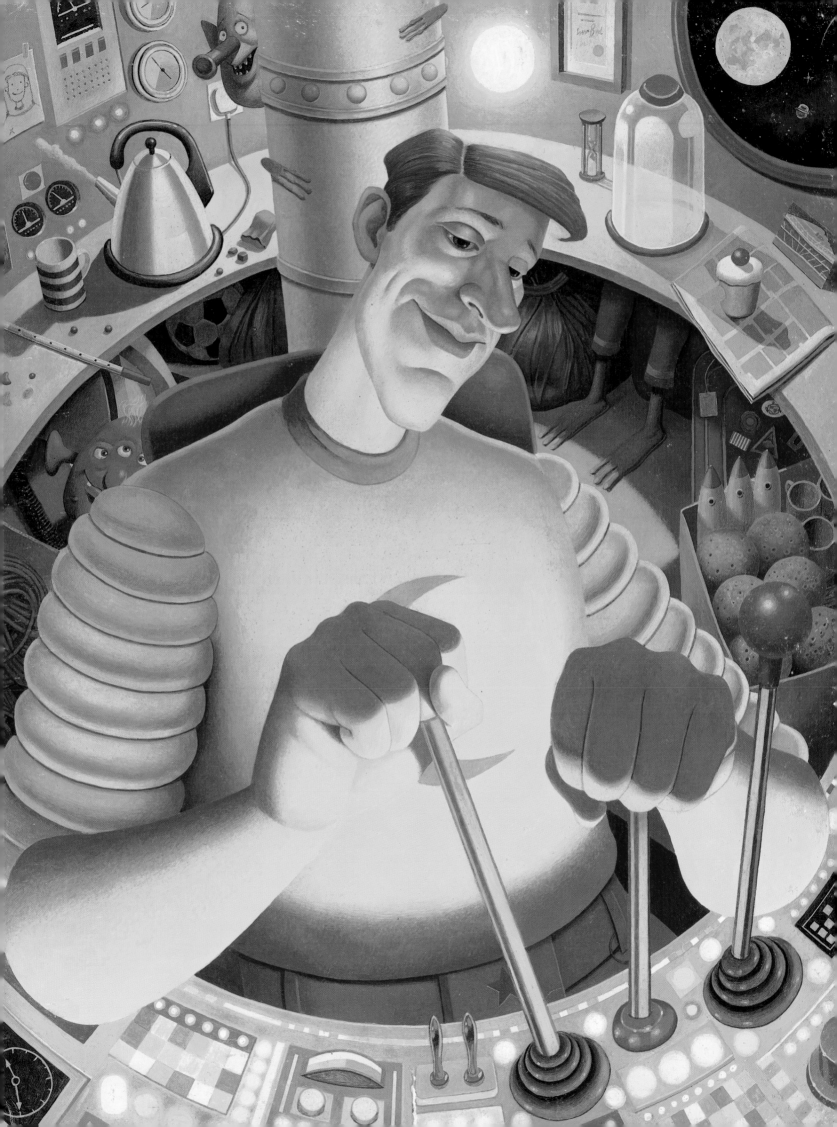

As he reaches Earth, it's about five o'clock.

The rush hour is in full swing with everyone leaving work and going home. Just like Bob.

When Bob gets home, first he has a long bath.
Moon work can make you very grubby because
sometimes the dust gets inside your suit.

At last Bob goes to bed with a mug of cocoa.
He sleeps soundly, bathed in moonbeams,
very happy to be the Man on the Moon.

And aliens . . . ?

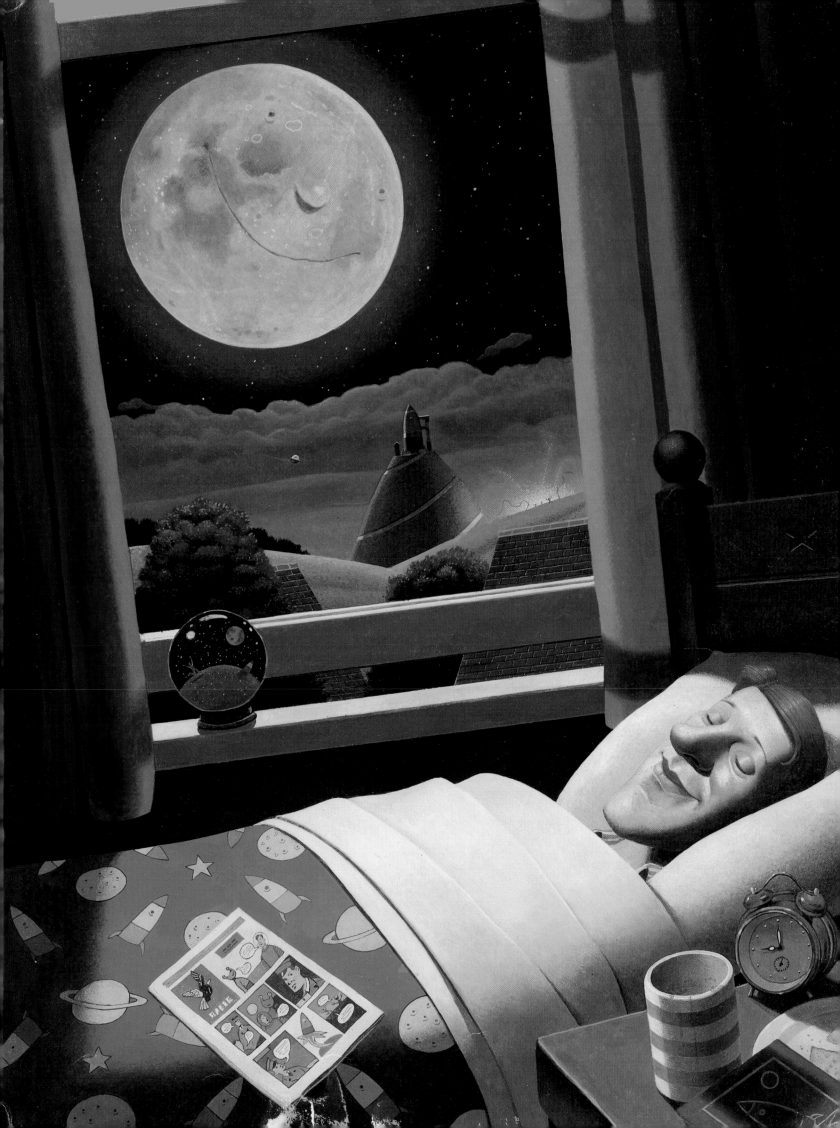

. . . wouldn't he?